This book was created for

To my little duck helpers J&L and
daddy Vaughan for your trees and patience

www.helenavaughan.co.uk

A duck on a river is where we begin,
swimming along and not fitting in.
With nowhere to go,
but go with the flow.

So he gave it some thought and went for a walk.

Duck took a walk down a busy little street.
All the way along, to see who he could meet.

Then a pigeon passed by,
so Duck said "Hi!"

"I'm looking for a place to go
where I don't feel alone.
I'm looking for a family.
A place to call my home."

"I live up in this tower,
so high up in the sky.
It gives a sense of power
over people passing by."

"Thank you and I love the view.
The problem is you see,
while it's just the place for you,
it's far too high for me."

Then Duck flew along a tree-lined street.
Way up in the branches, to see who he could meet.

When some bees buzzed by,
so Duck said "Hi!"

"I'm looking for a place to go
where I don't feel alone.
I'm looking for a family.
A place to call my home."

"We live here in this field.
It's simply like no other.
The thing that most appeals
to us is the stunning colour."

Then Duck took a walk down a narrow little path.
Round a bend,
    through a gate
        and straight into a park.

Then a dog ran by,
so Duck said "Hi!"

"I'm looking for a place to go
where I don't feel alone.
I'm looking for a family.
A place to call my home."

"WOOF!" said the dog
and ran around until
Duck got scared
and fell down a hill.

He climbed back up.

With a stroke of luck,
the dog ran away.

So Duck didn't stay!

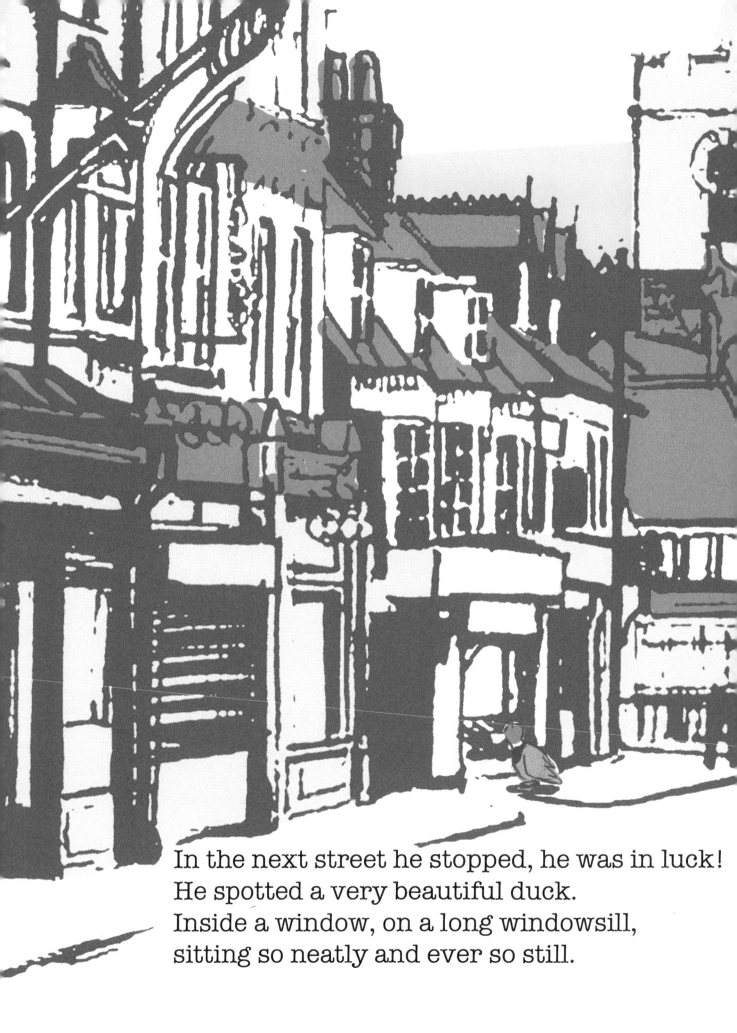

In the next street he stopped, he was in luck!
He spotted a very beautiful duck.
Inside a window, on a long windowsill,
sitting so neatly and ever so still.

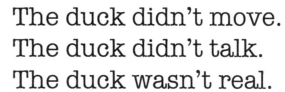

The duck didn't move.
The duck didn't talk.
The duck wasn't real.

So Duck turned to walk.

Our sad little duck then
found another park.
In through the gates
and he heard a small laugh.

"He he he!"

Then a squirrel whizzed by,
he stopped and said "Hi!"

"I'm looking for a place to go
where I don't feel alone.
I'm looking for a family.
A place to call my home."

"This park has a river
and plenty of trees.
So feel free to wander
wherever you please."

"Indeed I can see
it's got plenty of these.
But there must be more to
life, trees and water"

"Oh oh oh!
I know where to go!"
Said the squirrel so gladly
(and just slightly madly!)

So Duck found a family and somewhere to stay
No longer alone, this was duck's lucky day!

Lightning Source UK Ltd.
Milton Keynes UK
UKHW05f1047050618
323689UK00001B/8/P